Dick King-Smith

Emily's Legs

Illustrated by

Russell Ayto

Chapter One

To begin with, nobody noticed.

Mind you, you couldn't blame Mother Spider. If she'd only had one baby, she'd have been sure to notice.

But she had a hundred babies, all hatching out at the same time. How could she be expected to know that ninety-nine spiderlings were normal and one was different?

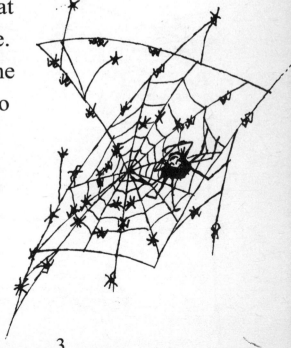

Father Spider didn't notice. For one thing, he didn't like children.

For another, he was always too busy sitting quite still, waiting for house-flies and bluebottles to land in his web, in the highest darkest corner of the room.

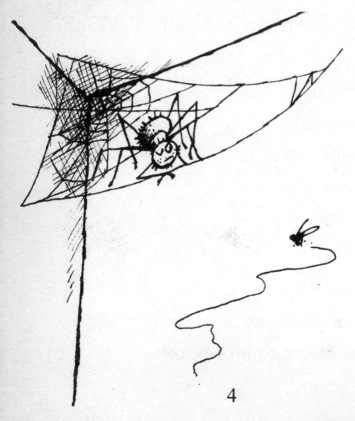

Emily's ninety-
nine brothers
and sisters
didn't notice.

Nobody noticed, not even Emily, until
the night of the Spider Sports.

For the grown-up
spiders, there were lots
of different events.
There was web-spinning
(how quickly could
you make a whole one
from start to finish) and

fly-parcelling
(how quickly
could you tie
up a fly in
silken threads)

and fly-eating (how quickly could you
. . . yes, well, I needn't explain that).

And there
was abseiling,
where you let out
a thread and
whizzed down it
from the ceiling,

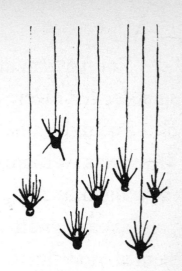

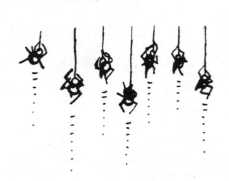

and thread-
climbing,
where you
whizzed
back up
again.

But for the spiderlings there were
only the eight-legged races.

Now this was where Emily's
troubles began.

Not that she didn't run in the
eight-legged races at the Spider Sports.
She did.
Not that she didn't win.
She did.
The trouble was that she won
them all and she won them all so easily.
First, all the spiderlings were
lined up at one end of the room, and
they had to race across the carpet to
the other end.

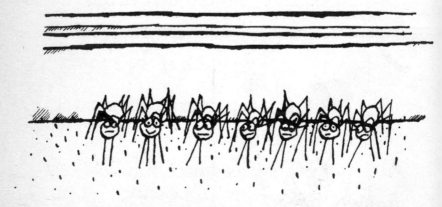

Emily won easily.

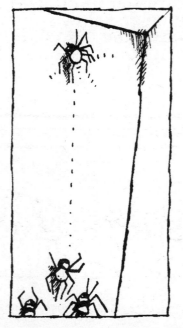

Then they had to race up the wall of the room.

Emily won easily.

9

Then they
had to race
down
the wall.

Emily won
easily.

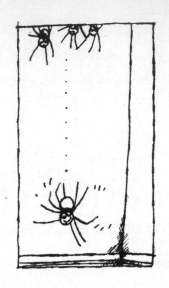

Last of all was the upside-down
eight-legged race, right across the
ceiling.

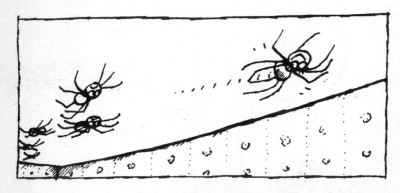

Yes, you've guessed, Emily won easily.

said all the grown-up spiders.

But the spiderlings weren't so happy.

they asked each other.

Why does Emily *always* win?

they asked the
grown-up spiders.

**Because
she's the
fastest,
of course**

said the grown-up spiders in the
knowing way that old folk have.

But *why*
is she the
fastest?

asked the spiderlings
in the annoying way
that young folk have.

12

And that was when the truth was discovered.

Emily was asked to appear in front of the Spider Sports Committee to receive her prizes – four neatly parcelled little flies.

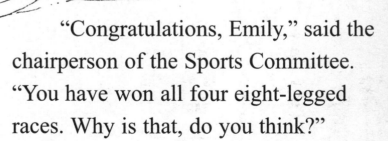

"Congratulations, Emily," said the chairperson of the Sports Committee. "You have won all four eight-legged races. Why is that, do you think?"

"If you please," said Emily (for she was by nature a polite spiderling), "it's because I ran the fastest."

"Ah!" said a very old grown-up spider. "But *why* did you run the fastest?"

Emily scratched her head with her two front legs. "I don't really know," she said modestly. "I suppose I just legged it quicker than they did."

"Legged it?" said the very old grown-up spider.

"Legged it?" said all the other grown-up spiders.

And they all looked carefully at
Emily's legs.

They weren't any different from
the legs of all the other spiderlings.

They were
no longer.

They
were no
stronger.

They were
no hairier.

But suddenly they all saw that,
though Emily was scratching her
head with her two front legs, she was
still standing on eight others.

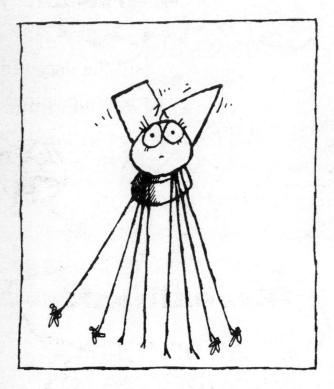

Emily had ten legs!

Chapter Two

For a moment nobody spoke.

Then . . .

Disgraceful!

said the very old grown-up spider.

Disgusting!

cried the chairperson of the Sports Committee.

Disqualified!

shouted all the other grown-up spiders.

Then Emily was made to hand
back the four neatly parcelled fly-prizes,
and the Committee scuttled off to spread
the news.

When Mother Spider heard it, she
went straight up the wall.

"Egbert!" she shouted. "Egbert!"
(for that was Father Spider's name)
"Where are you?"

Father Spider was
where he always was,
in the highest, darkest
corner of the room.

At first he did not answer.
His wife sounded angry. Like most
of his kind, he was a good deal smaller
than she was. A number of his old
friends had disappeared, suddenly
and completely, on account of their
wives being angry.

Or hungry.

Or both.

He tensed himself for a quick getaway, and as he saw his large wife approaching, he called out in a syrupy voice, "Why, Muriel," (for that was Mother Spider's name). "Whatever is the matter, dearest?"

"Oh Egbert!" cried Mother Spider. "It's Emily!"

"Who is Emily?"

"One of our children. Oh, the little wretch! Oh the shame! Oh, I'm so embarrassed!"

"Why?"

She has ten legs

said Mother Spider in a horrified voice.

Now as soon as Father Spider was sure that his wife was not angry with *him*, he changed his tune completely.

"Look here, Muriel," he said sternly. "First of all, you know that I don't like children. Second, I couldn't care less how many legs they have – she's lucky, this Emily, she's got a couple of spares. And third, I object to being interrupted when I'm busy."

"But you're not doing anything."

"Yes, I am. I'm busy sitting still, waiting for house-flies and bluebottles. Kindly go away!"

Meanwhile Emily sat silent, alone with her thoughts. She had counted her legs 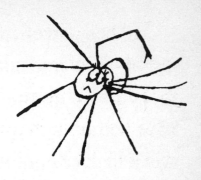 carefully, first clockwise, then anti-clockwise, but the answer came out the same either way – ten.

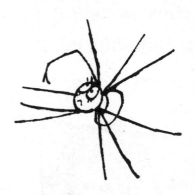 Emily felt sad, as anyone would who had been disqualified and had her prizes taken away and been shouted at by a Sports Committee.

And Mother and Father will be angry too, I suppose, she thought. Grown-ups! They're all the same.

Then she cheered up a bit. At least my brothers and sisters won't care, she thought. I'll go down to the Gym and have some fun. And off she scuttled (very fast, of course).

The Gym was an old dusty cupboard, where the spiderlings gathered to practise making their first very small webs, and to do abseiling and climbing and generally enjoy themselves.

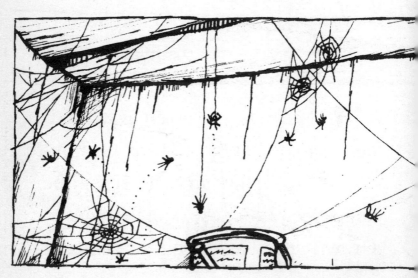

A number of large disused webs hung
across the cupboard, and these acted
as safety-nets for those who fell by
mistake, and trampolines for those who
fell on purpose.

Ten or a dozen spiderlings were
in the Gym when Emily arrived, but
the moment they saw her, they all
stopped doing whatever they were
doing and stared at her in silence.

Then one of them spoke.

"Cheat!" it said in a nasty voice.

"You're a cheat!"

And then the rest joined in.

"I didn't know," Emily said. "Honest, I didn't know I had ten," but they went on yelling, which made her angry.

"Anyway," she said, "I bet I could beat you lot with two legs tied behind my back."

At this, there was once again silence in the Gym. Then the first spiderling spoke again in a voice that was even nastier.

"You're never going to be given the chance," it said. "Come on, everybody. Get her!"

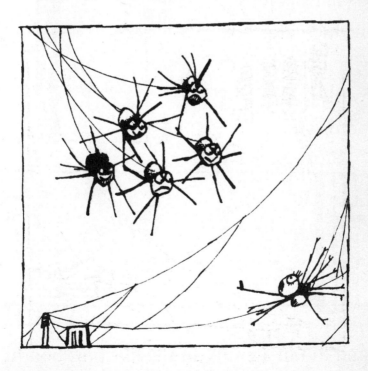

Chapter Three

Emily ran out of
the Gym as fast
as her ten legs
would carry her.
She ran down the
wall, dashed
across the carpet,

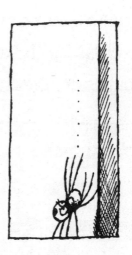

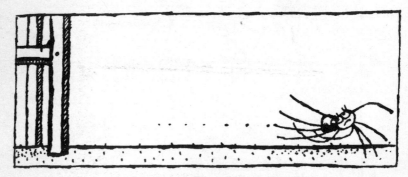

and hid in a crack in the skirting-board.

She waited, facing
outwards. The crack
was narrow, so that they
would only be able to
come at her one at a time.

"I'll jolly well show
'em," she said to herself.
"Calling me a cheat.
They'd better be careful."

She could hear the spiderlings chattering to each other as they ran about the room in search of her.

You just try it, thought Emily.
I'm not afraid of you.

But she was, and it was a great
relief to hear her mother's voice,
calling angrily to the others.

"What are you doing, naughty
children?" she cried to the gang of
spiderlings.

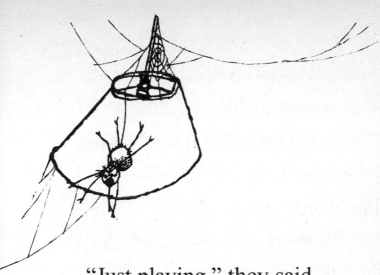

"Just playing," they said.

"How many times havc I told you not to play out in the room in broad daylight? Stay in the Gym, or under the chairs, or behind the curtains," said Mother Spider.

Then she used the threat that mother spiders everywhere use to frighten their naughty children.

"If you're not careful," she said, "the Hoover will get you! Now scuttle off, the lot of you!"

Emily waited till the spiderlings had gone, and then she came out of her hole. I'd better face the music, she thought. She can't eat me, after all. Or can she?

"Mother?" she said, a little nervously.

Mother Spider was hanging from the lampshade. She let out thread rapidly and came whizzing down to the floor. She did not look best pleased.

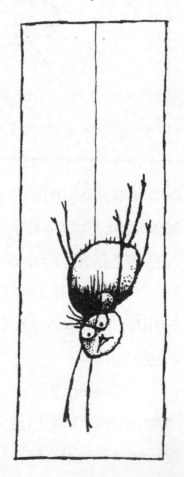

Emily crossed
two of her legs
for luck.
Mother Spider
walked all
round her
slowly. As
she went, she
counted out loud.

"So it's true," she said at last in a
low voice. "It's true what they're saying.
Never have I been so embarrassed."

"I didn't know, Mother," said
Emily. "Honest, I didn't know
I had ten."

"Nor did I," said Mother Spider.
"But now that I do, I've only one thing
to say to you."

"What's that?"

"Never darken my web again!"
said Mother Spider, and she
reeled in thread and shot up
into the lampshade
without a
backward
look.

Emily sighed. Perhaps my father will be kinder, she thought. She had never met him, but she knew where he lived.

She ran round the edge of the room, keeping a sharp eye out for other spiderlings, and began to climb to the highest darkest corner.

Father Spider was busy sitting still when he felt a slight shudder on his web. He dashed out, to find, not a house-fly or a bluebottle, but a spiderling.

"Father?" said Emily, a little nervously.

"Go away!" said Father Spider crossly. "You know I don't like children."

"But I'm your daughter."

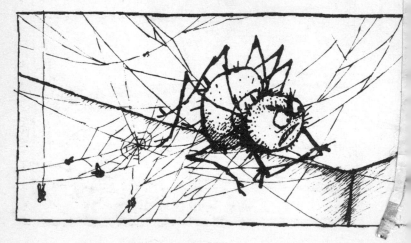

"I have hundreds of daughters,"
said Father Spider, "and hundreds of
sons, and I don't like any of them."

"But I'm Emily."

"The one with ten legs?"

"Yes," said Emily. "I didn't
know, Father," she said. "Honest,
I didn't know I had ten."

"What are you moaning about?"
said Father Spider. "Think yourself
lucky. You've got a couple of spares."

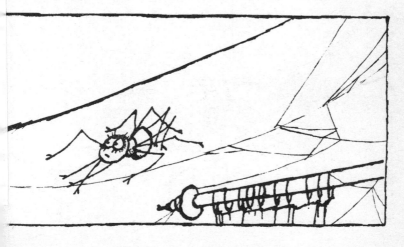

He pulled back the thread on which Emily was standing.

"Get lost!" he said, and he let it go with a twang.

Emily was hurled from the web like a stone from a catapult.

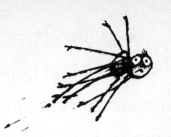

At the same time the room was filled with a sudden roaring noise, a noise that grew louder as Emily fell until, as she hit the floor, it was very loud indeed.

And very close.

Dazed and helpless, Emily could only watch as the monster rushed towards her.

Her mother's words echoed in her brain. "The Hoover will get you!"

Chapter Four

In time to come, when Emily was herself a mother spider, her own spiderlings often asked her for a web-time story. And their favourite was "The Day The Hoover Ate Mum".

They knew, because they had heard it so often, that it had a happy ending.

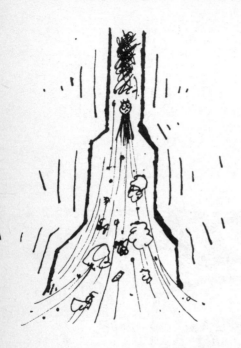

But a happy ending was the last thing Emily expected when she was sucked into the mouth of the vacuum cleaner. The first thing she felt was a sharp pain (two sharp pains, to be exact).

Then she found herself in a thick choking blackness, unable to see or to cry out – for her eyes and mouth were full of dust – and unable to hear anything but the dreadful deafening noise of the machine. For a moment, Emily thought she was dead.

But then the Hoover was switched off, the heap of fluff and dirt settled to the bottom of the bag, and Emily fought her way to the top of it.

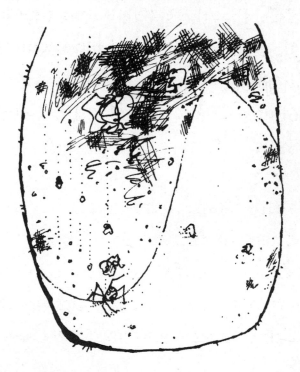

To her surprise and relief she
found she was not alone, for suddenly
a voice rang out in the darkness.

"All clear, my lads!" it cried.
"Us can unroll now."

Once her eyes had grown
accustomed to the darkness, Emily
could see that the speaker was a large
woodlouse, and that several other
woodlice had climbed to the top of the
pile of dust. They looked at Emily in
a friendly manner.

"Hullo, young 'un," said the
first woodlouse. "You'm looking a
bit gloomy."

"I am," said Emily. "Nobody likes
me. Not my mother nor my father nor
my horrid brothers and sisters."

"Whyever not?"

"Because I've got ten legs."

"Poor little mite!" cried the
woodlouse. "Only ten!"

"Why d'you say 'only' ten?"
said Emily.

"Because you should have
fourteen by rights. All woodlice has
fourteen legs."

"But she's not a woodlouse," said
a voice behind Emily. "She's a spider."

Emily turned round to see a
spiderling, a little smaller than herself,
emerging from the dust-pile.

"Who are you?" she said.

"My name's James," said the spiderling. "What's yours?"

"Emily," said Emily. "I hope you're not one of my brothers?"

"I hope not," said James. "They don't sound very nice."

"They're not," said Emily. "They're horrible to me. And so are my sisters. And so are my mother and father."

"What are your parents' names?" said James.

"Muriel and Egbert."

"Never heard of them."

"Good. Then you can't be related to me."

"No," said James. "But when we get out of here, I'd like to be," and he put one of his legs round Emily's waist.

"Oh don't be so soppy!" cried Emily, pushing him away. "Anyway, we're never going to get out of here."

"Oh yes you will, young 'un!" cried the woodlice.

"All you got to do is wait . . ."

". . . till they empties the Hoover bag . . ."

". . . into the dustbin . . ."

". . . and then you climbs up the inside of it . . ."

". . . and the next time they do take the lid off . . ."

". . . out you pops!"

"But when will they empty it?" said Emily.

"Soon, I should think," said James. "It's pretty full," and hardly were the words out of his mouth when they all felt the Hoover being lifted, and carried away, and set down again.

Then they heard the zip of the outer cover being undone, and the thick paper bag in which they were all imprisoned shook.

"Watch out, my lads!" shouted the first woodlouse. "We'm a-going!"

"Quickly, Emily," said James. "Attach safety-lines!"

He was only just in time, because at that moment the bottom of the paper bag was opened, and dirt and dust and fluff and woodlice fell into the dustbin.

The bag
was empty,
save for the
two spiderlings
suspended
within it; and
before it could
be closed again
Emily and

James let out thread, swung themselves
to the side of the dustbin, and
scampered up the wall of it and over
the rim and away.

They scuttled for the nearest cover
and crouched there breathlessly till all
was quiet again.

Then James began to stare at
Emily's legs.

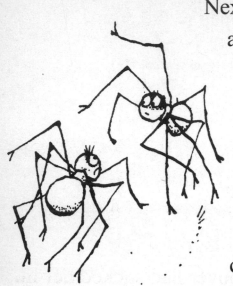

Next, he walked
all round her
slowly. As
he went, he
counted out
loud.
"Oh don't
you start!"
cried Emily.
"If you don't
like me having ten
legs, you can jolly well push off!"

James stopped at the count
of eight.

"You haven't," he said.

"Haven't what?"

"Haven't got ten legs. You've got
eight. Same as any other spider."

And then Emily remembered the
sharp pain (two sharp pains, to be
exact) as the Hoover had sucked her in.

"Except you're not the same as
any other spider, Emily," said James.
"You're prettier. I think it would be
nice if we set up web together," and
once again he put one of his legs round
Emily's waist.

"Oh don't be so soppy!" cried
Emily. But this time she did not push
him away.

"And anyway," said James, "they'll grow again."

"What will?"

"The two legs you lost. Spiders of our sort can do that."

"How d'you know?"

"My dad's done it. Mum lost her

temper with him and pulled off one of
his, and he grew a lovely new one."

"Gosh!" said Emily excitedly.
"Then I'll still be the fastest spider of
them all!"

"Yes."

"But oh!" said Emily miserably.
"You won't like me any more, James.
Not with ten legs."

"Emily," said James. "When legs are as beautiful as yours, you cannot possibly have too many of them," and he stroked one of hers with one of his.

"Oh James!" said Emily happily. "You say the soppiest things!"

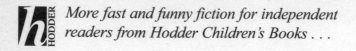
More fast and funny fiction for independent readers from Hodder Children's Books . . .

Dick King-Smith

Henry Pond
THE POET

Illustrated by
Russell Ayto

Henry Pond is a toad.
He's also a poet.
His poems are famous, and he has many
proud fans. Sadly, Victoria Garden-Pool
isn't one of them. She prefers Larry Lake
– a toad of action, not words.

But Henry's determined to win over
this warty beauty. Can his brains beat
Larry's brawn?